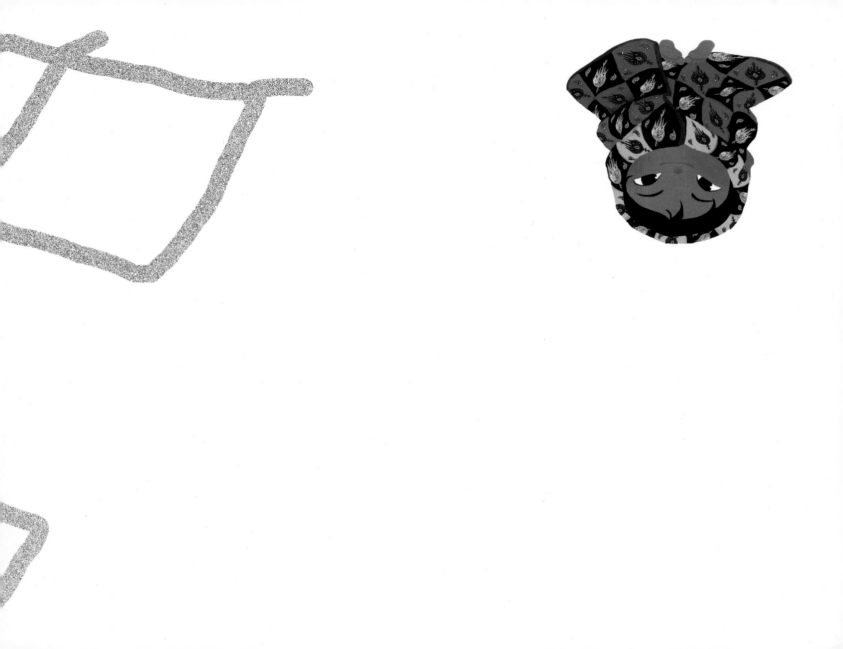

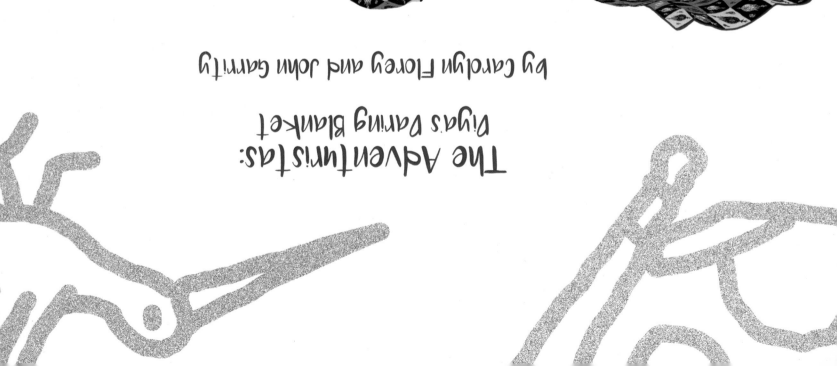

The Adventuristas:
Riya's Daring Blanket

by Carolyn Florey and John Garrity

ISBN 978-1-7327544-2-3

Library of Congress Cataloging-in-Publication Data is available.

Visit www.TheAdventuristasBooks.com

To our parents –
thank you for always encouraging and
supporting our adventures

Special thanks to our close friends who provided guidance
on cultural and language references in this book

Amma* wraps my favorite blanket around me so tight.
I'm warm and cozy, trying with all of my might,
To remember the snowballs thrown in the field.
A snow fortress built to act as our shield.

Shadow animals flicker on the wall,
Lamplights make them seem so tall.

*Amma is a common way to say mother
across languages in southern India

And then I'm back in the park, sledding down the hills.
I was scared at first, but by force of my will,
I kept going and going, trying something new,
Weeeeee down the hill, then whooosh and then wooooooooo!!!

But wait, where'd I go? I can't see my feet!
They've disappeared under this blanket, oh what a treat!
An invisibility cloak, the rarest of finds.
I'll tiptoe around and never you mind.
No one can see me, not even a clue,
That I'm right behind here following you.

Whose hand is that?

Whose foot?

And whose arm?

I'll explore many places and do no harm.
Leave a treat here, a helping hand there,
Surprising Paati* with some flowers I bear.

* Paati is short for Paatima and means grandmother in Tamil

And then I'm visible, in plain sight,
Standing on the pitcher's mound, winding up tight.

Throwing the ball right across home plate,
Leaving my fingertips, feeling the fate.

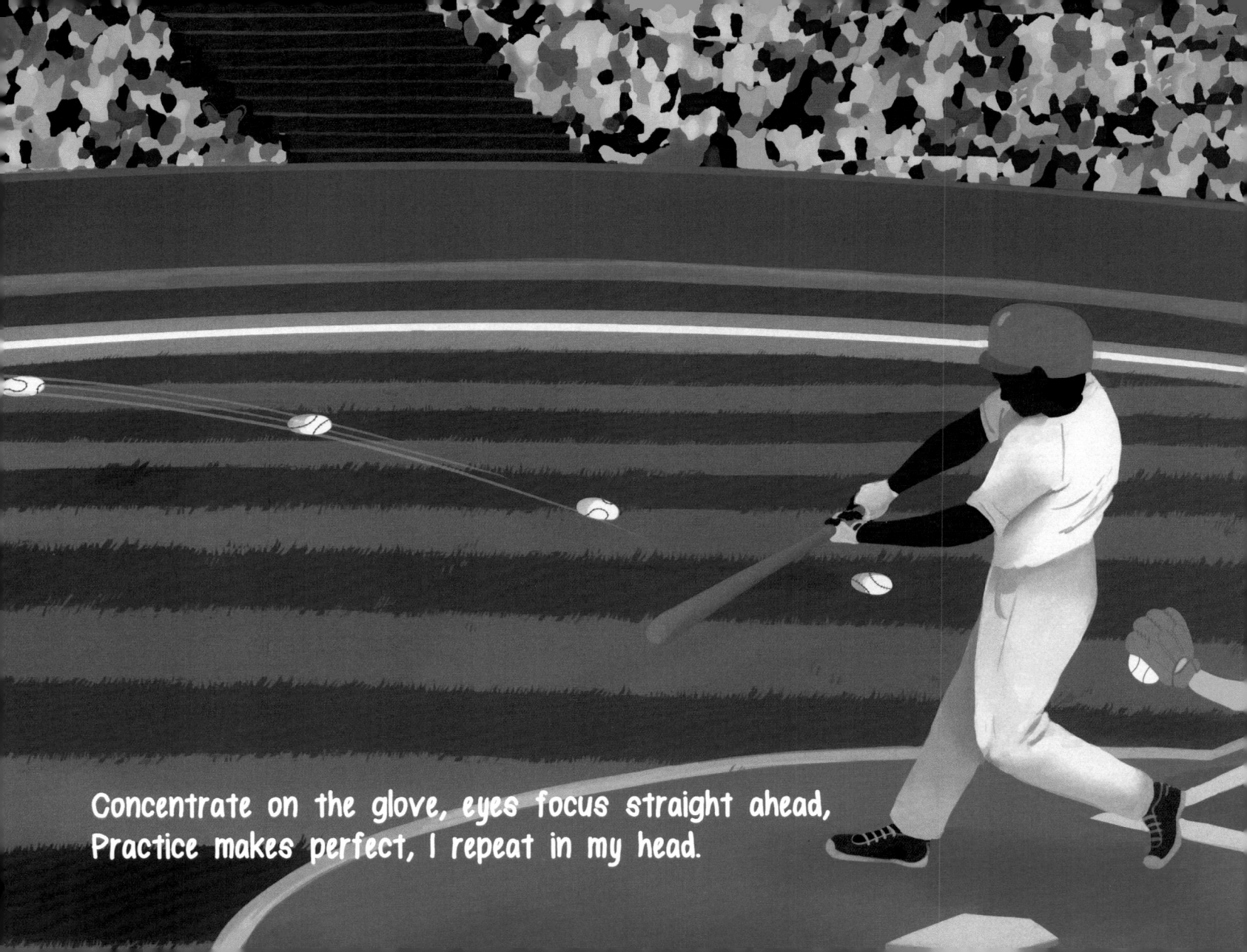

Concentrate on the glove, eyes focus straight ahead,
Practice makes perfect, I repeat in my head.

Striiiiike THREE and it's over, the game winning pitch!!
Three up and three down, without even a hitch.
I hoot and holler, jump up in the air,
Then wait, where'd I go, I see a waterfall there!

Wearing a life jacket, water is gushing
Close by and I can feel my adrenaline rushing.
We are down in Brazil, in the middle of nature,
See the water, the trees, and all of the creatures.

From the falls to the grass, with Thatha* by my side,
Doing yoga each day, the time just floats by.
Breathe in and breathe out, clear our minds and our hearts,
Me and Thatha together, never to part!

*Thatha means grandfather in Tamil

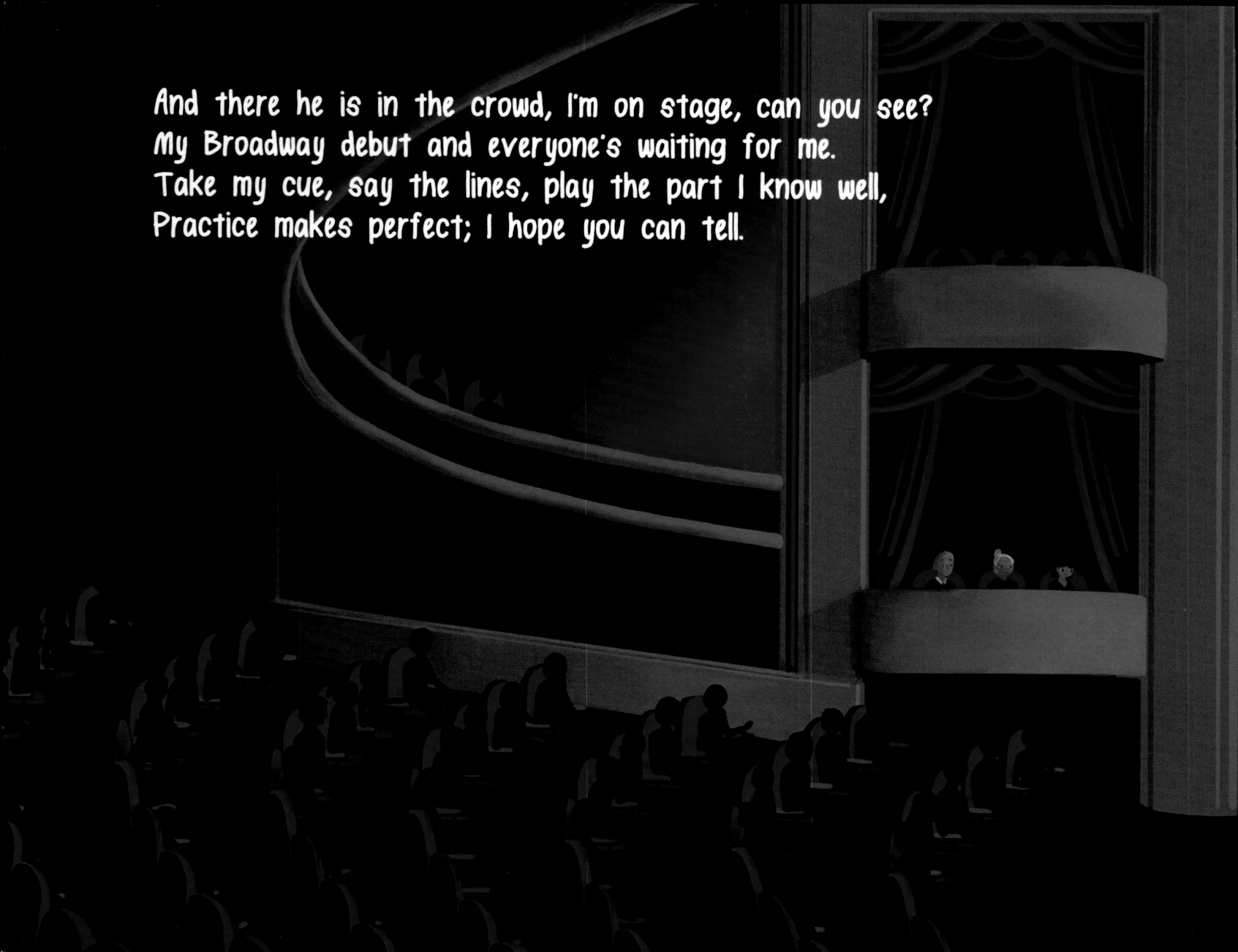

And there he is in the crowd, I'm on stage, can you see?
My Broadway debut and everyone's waiting for me.
Take my cue, say the lines, play the part I know well,
Practice makes perfect; I hope you can tell.

Take a bow, blow a kiss, wave hands high in the air,
What a joy entertaining, I don't have a care.

Then whoosh comes the blanket, taking me away,
I look back one more time at the end of the play.

A magic carpet, what fun! It's taking me higher!
We soar with the eagle, flying right beside her.
here's Honest Abe in D.C. and Saint Basil's in Moscow,
The Eiffel Tower in Paris — up, up we go!

Watch the herds of wildebeest migrate across the Serengeti,
The Taj Mahal is a teardrop on the face of eternity.

The orangutans swing from trees in the forest.
Look at his hands and feet - they are just like us!

Then off to Machu Picchu, the ancient Incan city,
Can't believe I'm flying high, the world looks so itty-bitty.

With one fell swoop, I'm on a camping trip,
making yummy s'mores as the marshmallows drip!
Appa* plays guitar and sings into the night;
Ghost stories are told, oh what a fright!

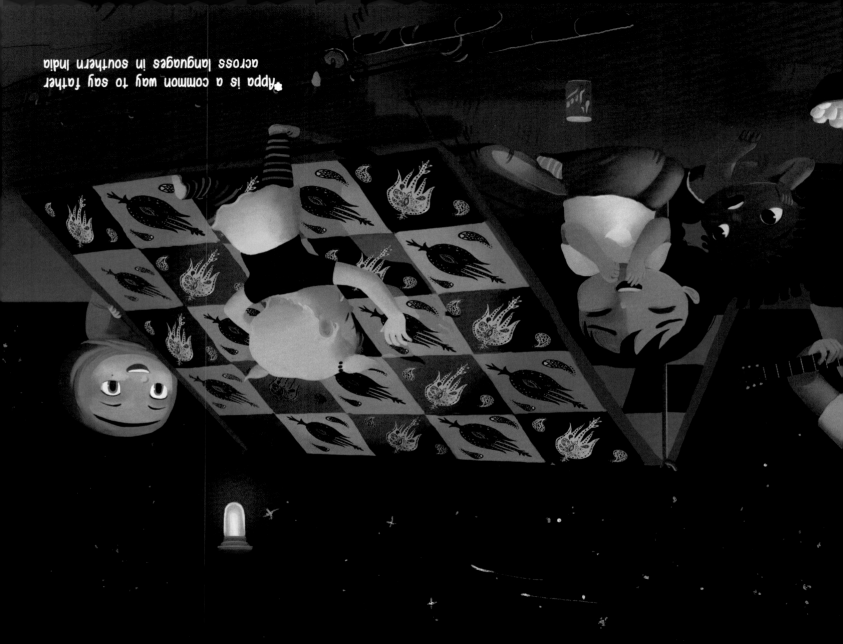

*Appa is a common way to say father across languages in southern India

Off we go again, up up and we soar,
Paragliding is freeing, I'm begging for more.
I feel free as a bird as we sail on the wind,
The snow-capped mountains go on forever, without any end.

We land safe on the hill and wait, who am I?
Super Adventurista to the rescue as I sail through the sky!

So teeny and tiny you can't see a thing;
Save the planet from trash and then I will bring

From Super Adventurista to super daughter, it's time to get dressed. Amma and I wear the colors that we like the best.

Her beautiful sari flows with such grace,
Wrap it around and around, you need lots of space!

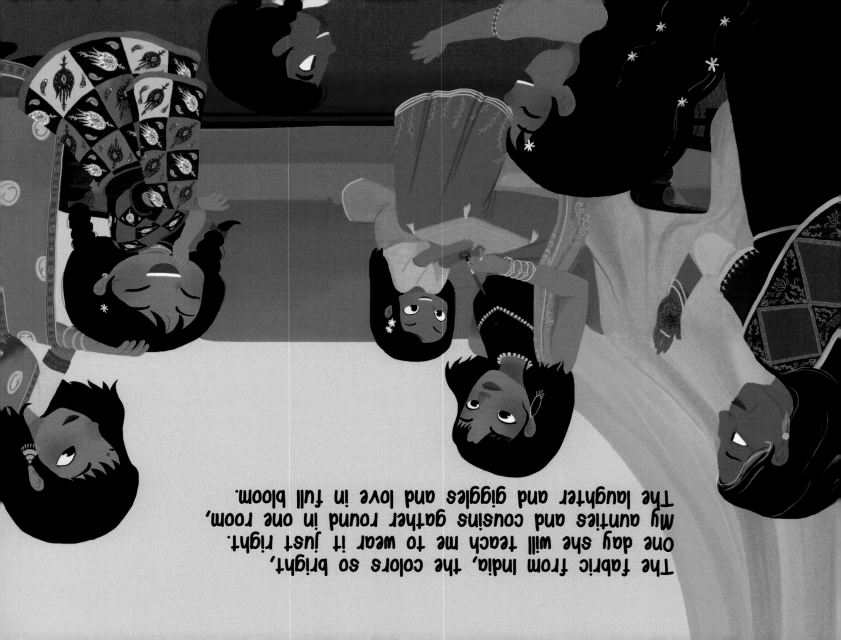

The fabric from India, the colors so bright,
one day she will teach me to wear it just right.
My aunties and cousins gather round in one room,
The laughter and giggles and love in full bloom.

More adventures we will have together I know,
I'll be just like my Amma when I start to grow.
But now it's time for some soup in my belly,
Transporting me back from auntie's house in New Delhi.

And now it's time for me to say,
WHAT WAS YOUR ADVENTURE TODAY?